The
Child
Willow Green

The Children at Willow Green

MARJORIE NEWMAN

Illustrated by Joanna Williams

Scripture Union
130 City Road, London EC1V 2NJ

By the same author
Party Day

Phototypeset by Input Typesetting Ltd, London
Printed and bound in Great Britain by Cox and
Wyman Ltd Reading

Contents

1 **Peter**   9
Thank you, God, because we can make
things

2 **Anna**   14
Telling the truth is best

3 **Fifty dozen friends**   19
It's fun to make other people happy

4 **Margaret**   24
God cares how we feel

5 **Windy day**   28
We can't see God but he's real

6 **Harvest**   33
Thank you, God, for harvest

7 **James**   38
God helps us when we're afraid

8 **Class One's assembly**   43
Thank you, God, for water

9 **Richard**   47
   Doing *our* part

10 **Christmas**   52
   It's fun to give at Christmas

11 **Jonathan**   57
   Thank you, God, for books and reading

12 **Birthday surprise**   62
   Thank you, God, for birthdays

13 **Okolo**   67
   God cares about us

14 **Heidi**   72
   God wants us to be helpful

15 **Derek**   77
   God wants us to make others welcome

16 **Sports day**   81
   Different people are good at different
   things

17 **The wildlife park**   86
   God made a wonderful world

18 **Janice**   91
   We can be sure of God's love

Peter

It was Class One's fourth morning at Willow Green School. Peter stood at the classroom window, watching his mum go across the playground. At the school gate she turned round and waved to him. Then she was gone.

Behind him, the other children in Class One were getting out the toys they had chosen. They seemed to like school already. The room felt very noisy, and full of people. Peter wished it was home time . . .

Mrs Dixon came over.

'Peter, love – what would you like to do this morning?' she asked. Peter looked at her; but he couldn't think of anything to say. She smiled, and held out her hand.

'Come on. Let's have a look round!' she said.

Peter went with her.

'What about a jigsaw puzzle?' she asked. Class One had some lovely jigsaw puzzles. Peter nodded. Mrs Dixon picked the jungle one out for him, and sat him down at a table. Peter looked at the puzzle. You could take the animals out and play with them separately, if you wanted to.

Slowly, Peter lifted out a monkey. Paul came by in his wheelchair. 'I can do that puzzle!' he said. Peter put the monkey back again. It made him feel shy when the other children talked about what he was doing.

Paul had gone on; but Peter didn't take out any more

animals, because now Okolo and Pavan had come to sit at his table. He watched them building with little bricks, and wondered if it would be nice to join in. But he couldn't think how to say it.

Presently Mrs Dixon came over to him again.

'What about playing with the sand?' she suggested. 'Come and try!'

Peter went with her, although he knew he didn't want to be at the sand-tray. There were always other children there, and sometimes they got excited and snatched each other's spades or measuring cups. As soon as Mrs Dixon left him, he sat down on the nearest chair – which happened to be right at the back of the room, against the wall. He felt safer there, because no one was noticing him.

But before too long Mrs Dixon saw him.

'Oh, *Peter*!' she said, with a smile. 'I tell you what – you sit there and have a nice time watching the others this morning. Because I think *tomorrow* you'll want to join in.'

Peter didn't say anything; but he felt a bit better. Maybe he *would* want to join in tomorrow.

From where he sat he could see the children at the painting table. They weren't talking much. They were getting on with their pictures – big pictures, on huge pieces of paper. At the end of the morning they'd be able to take their pictures home . . .

The next morning Peter stood at the window again, waving goodbye to Mum. Then he went and stood by the painting table.

Mrs Dixon came hurrying over. But she only said, 'Shall I help you on with an overall, Peter?'

Peter nodded.

As soon as the painting overall was on, Mrs Dixon found him a piece of paper and made sure he was settled.

Only Jivan was at the table, so there was plenty of room. Then she went away to help someone else.

Peter picked up a paintbrush from the red jar. He looked across at Jivan. Jivan was busily painting a ship, and not noticing Peter at all.

Carefully, Peter made one long red line on his piece of paper. *Great*! He got more paint on the brush, and made another red line, crossing the first one. Splendid! He got a lot of paint on the brush, and made lots of red lines, all criss-crossing each other. He put the red brush back, picked up the blue one, and made some beautiful blue lines. Where they crossed the red ones the paint turned purple. Peter grinned. He put the blue brush back, and took out the green one . . .

By the time Mrs Dixon came to see what he was doing, the paper was full of painted lines of all colours.

'That's lovely, Peter!' she said. 'You *have* been busy! Would you like another piece of paper now?'

'Yes please,' said Peter.

This time he painted a house, with Mum and Dad and Moggy the cat and himself all inside it. There was only just room.

At lunch-time he rushed out of school carrying his paintings. Mum had come to meet him. She thought they were the best paintings she'd ever seen.

And when Dad saw them, at tea-time, *he* thought so too. He stuck them up on the wall in the kitchen because he said they would cheer him up in the morning while he was eating his breakfast.

Peter felt very happy. He helped with clearing away the tea things, and with the washing up. Then he watched Mum getting out her pastry board.

'I'm going to make some cakes this evening, so that they'll be ready for Gran when she comes tomorrow,' Mum said. 'I shan't have time in the morning.'

'Can I make some cakes too?' Peter asked.

'Of course you can,' said Mum.

As they set to work Mum said, 'I've made several things today, Pete. I finished knitting your pullover. And I made a new bed for Mog – her cardboard box was all torn.'

'And you made dinner, and tea,' said Peter. Mum laughed.

'So I did!' she agreed. 'And you made your paintings–'

'And a Plasticine dinosaur!' said Peter. 'And a paper tiger. I like making things!'

'I'm glad God gave us hands that can manage it!' said Mum. 'And heads that can think of the way to do it!'

'So'm I!' said Peter.

'So'm I!' said Dad, who had heard what they were saying.

Peter laughed. But that night they all said a special thank-you to God – because it was so nice to be able to make things.

Anna

Anna hopped happily along the corridor beside Mrs Dixon. At *last* Class One were going to be allowed to use the school library. They would be able to choose a book to take home! Anna couldn't wait!

The library was in a small room next to the hall. There were shelves of books all round the walls. When Class One went in, they saw Okolo's mother sitting at the table in the corner. She smiled at them. Okolo waved. But there wasn't time to talk just then.

'Remember, children,' Mrs Dixon was saying, 'our class can choose any of the books which have a red square on the cover. When you've chosen, take the book over to Okolo's mummy. She kindly comes in each week to help us with the library. She has a card for each of you in that special box.'

Anna looked at the box, and wriggled excitedly. Mrs Dixon went on, 'Okolo's mummy will write the name of the book on your library card. When you bring the book back, she'll put a tick by its name. Then you can choose your next book. At the end of the term, we'll know just which books you've had! And you'll have one of these plastic folders to carry the books in. Now – are you ready?'

'Yes!' yelled Class One.

'Then off you go!' Mrs Dixon smiled. 'Carefully! The

books won't run away!'

Giggling, the children began to choose. Anna picked a story about cats. When everyone was ready, Mrs Dixon said, 'Now listen, children! This is important!'

Class One was very quiet. Mrs Dixon said, 'Remember – you're only allowed to borrow these books if you take care of them! You must *not* lose them! And no one wants to read a book which is torn or dirty, either! Do you understand?'

'Yes, Mrs Dixon,' said Class One.

'And do you promise to take great care of them?' she asked.

'Yes, Mrs Dixon,' they promised. Anna promised loudest of all.

At home-time she was first out of the school gate, waving her book so that Mum could see. And as soon as she got home, she sat down to look at the book properly.

Dad came in. When he'd had his tea, he read the story to her. And at bedtime, Mum read it to her again. Anna could read some of the words herself.

She had that story every bedtime until library day came round again. Then Mum carried the book in its folder for her. At the school gate Mum kissed her good-bye, gave her the book, and went off to do the shopping.

'Come and play, Anna!' called some of the others. Anna put the book down carefully on a seat, and ran to join them.

The bell rang, and the children hurried into school. Anna hung up her coat, and went into the classroom beside Paul in his wheelchair, talking and laughing.

It wasn't until she was sitting on the carpet waiting for the register to be called that Anna noticed something. Most of the other children were holding their library books . . . Anna's book was still out in the playground.

15

She went cold all over. She'd promised to take special care of the book – and now she'd left it outside! Mrs Dixon would be very, very cross.

Perhaps if Anna didn't *say* anything, Mrs Dixon wouldn't find out. When playtime came, Anna could go and get it.

Mrs Dixon called the register. Then she said, 'All the children who've brought their library book back, come out here.'

Anna sat still.

'Not you, Anna?' asked Mrs Dixon in surprise. She knew how much Anna liked books. Anna went very red, and shook her head.

'All right,' said Mrs Dixon. 'Children, put your books safely on my table for now. Presently we'll go along to the library.'

Anna watched the other children putting their books in a pile. She wished hers was there.

And then the door opened and Miss Westmore, the headmistress, walked into the room. She was frowning. In her hand she held Anna's library book.

'Who was careless enough to leave this book in the playground?' asked Miss Westmore.

Anna felt *terrible*. But she *couldn't* make herself speak.

'Come along!' said Miss Westmore. 'Remember, I can easily find out by looking at the cards in the library box!'

Anna began to cry.

'Anna!' said Mrs Dixon, in surprise.

And Miss Westmore said, 'It was you, Anna, was it?' Not daring to look up, Anna nodded.

'Well!' said Miss Westmore. 'I always thought you were a very careful little girl!'

'She *is* very careful usually,' said Mrs Dixon. 'I'm sure she'll never leave a library book about again.'

'I hope not,' said Miss Westmore. 'As it is, Anna, I

can't let you borrow any more books for two weeks. Do you understand?'

'Yes,' sobbed Anna.

Miss Westmore went out, taking Anna's book with her. Class One was very quiet, except for the sound of Anna's crying. They watched as Mrs Dixon came over, picked Anna up, and sat her on her lap.

'I'm sorry this has happened,' Mrs Dixon said. 'I'm sorry Anna won't be able to borrow another book for two weeks. But does anyone know what I'm most sorry about?'

Class One tried to guess. But no one guessed right.

'I'm most sorry that she didn't tell me the truth when I asked her if she'd brought her book back today,' Mrs Dixon said. 'Imagine what the world would be like if we never knew whether people were telling us the truth or not!'

Anna tried to imagine it. It would be *dreadful*.

'I'm s-sorry,' she whispered.

Mrs Dixon gave her a comforting squeeze.

'Then we'll say no more about it. But I tell you what, Class One! I want each of you to draw me a picture about telling the truth. You can make it someone who *is*, or someone who *isn't*. Then we'll talk. Right! Off you go!'

And Class One hurried to get paper and crayons.

Fifty dozen friends

The children in Class One were listening to their teacher, Mrs Dixon. She was telling them something special.

'You've all been in school for three weeks now,' she smiled. 'Next week we're having an Open Day. Do you know what that means?'

The children shook their heads.

'It means your mums and dads and aunties and uncles and grans and grandads can come and visit us!' she said. 'It's not so that they can talk to me about you. We'll have an evening for that, later on – when I know you better! It's so that they can look round the school, and see the children in their new classes.'

Class One began to feel excited.

'Now,' said Mrs Dixon, 'If you're going to have special visitors at home, what do you do?'

'Tidy up!' said Class One.

'Right,' said Mrs Dixon. 'We'll make sure everything is nice and tidy for next Friday. But we'll do even more than that. We'll try to make the whole room look very interesting. We'll have your paintings pinned up on the walls. And perhaps we'll have some of the words you can write up there, as well. And some of your tracings. And we'll have some of your number work to show – and some of the junk models you've been making – oh, there are lots of things we'll do! So we shall all be very busy from now until then! Today I want us to think mainly about making pictures.'

Excitedly, Class One set to work.

'I'm going to paint! I'm painting a big dragon!' cried Richard, as he rushed to the painting table.

'So'm I!' shouted Heidi, rushing after him.

'You can't!' said Richard. 'I said it first!'

'I can!' said Heidi. 'Mrs Dixon – I *can* do a dragon, can't I!'

Mrs Dixon came over to them. 'Everyone can paint whatever picture they choose,' she explained. 'But it would be nice to have as many different pictures as possible.'

'My dragon *will* be different!' said Heidi. 'It will be the best,' she added.

Mrs Dixon sighed. She left them, and went to see why Paul was reaching down so low he was almost falling out of his wheelchair. Paul couldn't walk, so he sat in his wheelchair most of the time; but it didn't stop him from doing what the others did.

'I'm trying to get a piece of blue paper,' he said now. The blue paper was at the bottom of the pile.

'Margaret! You were right here! Couldn't you see Paul needed a piece of blue paper?' asked Mrs Dixon.

Margaret looked up from the yellow piece she had pulled out for herself, and shook her head. Mrs Dixon sighed again. She handed Paul a piece of blue paper, and went over to Pavan, who was nearly crying.

'I can't do it!' he was saying.

'Can't do what?' asked Mrs Dixon.

'Anything nice,' said Pavan.

'Pavan, of course you can!' she said. 'You made a beautiful Plasticine model yesterday, for one thing! I'll show you how to make a Plasticine picture, if you like!'

Pavan looked a bit happier. He went to fetch some

Plasticine. Mrs Dixon helped him for a minute or two. Then she hurried over to a group of children who were tugging at a box of crayons.

'I got them first!' they were all shouting.

'Children!' she said sharply. 'Stop that! You'll spill them.'

Next moment the crayons tipped up and scattered all over the floor.

'Now pick them up before everyone treads on them!' said Mrs Dixon crossly. She looked around the room. Instead of the happy faces she usually saw, the children were frowning and squabbling.

When the crayons were back in their box with only two trodden on and squashed, Mrs Dixon clapped her hands for silence. Class One looked at her.

'Children,' she said, 'you're getting this all wrong! You're just thinking about what *you* are going to do, and how *your* piece of work will be the best! That's not the way. When we have visitors we try to think of what *they* will like. We want to make it a nice day for *them*! Of *course* we want your best work to show them! But we don't want a miserable crowd of children! Now do we?'

'No,' said Class One.

'That wouldn't make a happy day!' said Mrs Dixon. 'So – let's get on. But let's help each other, the way we usually do!'

Class One thought for a moment. Then they nodded.

'I'll get the brush and sweep up the crayon bits!' said Okolo.

'Can I do the flowers for you, Mrs Dixon?' asked Heidi.

'Can I take the register to Miss Westmore's room?' asked Estelle.

'Can I tidy up the jigsaw puzzles for you?' asked Jonathan.

'Can I tidy the book corner?' cried Naima.

'Can I – ' began six other people.

'Stop, stop!' laughed Mrs Dixon, putting her hands over her ears. 'Now I feel as if I've got fifty *dozen* helpers!'

Okolo looked round at everyone.

'Fifty dozen friends!' he said.

Mrs Dixon took her hands away from her ears, and smiled at him. 'Good boy, Okolo! That's exactly it! We're all friends! And we're going to have a lovely time next Friday!'

'Yes!' shouted Class One.

That evening they took home the letters reminding their parents about the Open Day. At school they worked hard so that their room would be welcoming. And they tried to do their best work so that the visitors would be pleased.

All the children were very excited on Open Day. Lots of grown-ups came, as well as their own mums and dads and aunties and uncles and grandparents. Most of the grown-ups said how clever the children in Class One were. But even more of them said how nice and friendly it felt in their room.

'Yes!' beamed Okolo. 'Fifty dozen friends!'

And Class One laughed.

Margaret

Margaret stood holding on to the school gate, screaming. The other children going into school looked at her in surprise. But Mum looked at her crossly.

'Margaret! Don't be so silly! You like school – you know you do! So come along in!'

'No!' screamed Margaret. 'No! No! No!'

'Margaret's a naughty girl, isn't she, Mum!' said Margaret's little sister Diana.

'I'm not! I'm not!' yelled Margaret.

'Yes, you are,' said Diana.

'Stop it, Diana! Stop it, *both* of you!' said Mum. 'Margaret – here comes your *teacher* now!'

Margaret stopped screaming for a moment to look at Mrs Dixon. Then she started again, louder than ever.

Mrs Dixon spoke quietly to Mum.

'Has anything happened at school to upset her?'

'I don't think so,' said Mum, very worried. 'She hasn't told us anything. And she seems very happy here.'

'She's naughty!' said Diana.

'Diana!' snapped Mum. And Margaret kicked out at her sister. '*Margaret!*' cried Mum.

'All right,' said Mrs Dixon. 'I'll take Margaret into school. Don't worry!'

So Mum took Diana off down the road.

As soon as Mum had gone, Margaret stopped screaming. Mrs Dixon held out a hand to her.

'Come on! In we go!'

They went into school together. Mrs Dixon helped Margaret to take her coat off and hang it up in the cloakroom. They went into the classroom, and Mrs Dixon settled Margaret on the carpet.

When the register had been called, and all the other children were busy, Mrs Dixon took Margaret onto her lap and tried to find out what was the matter. But Margaret wouldn't say. So in the end Mrs Dixon let her begin a painting, and everything seemed all right.

But back at home, Diana was screaming.

'I don't *want* any orange juice! And I don't want to play with those stupid dolls! And I don't want – '

'Diana,' said Mum, 'if you're not careful I shall put you to bed, whether you want it or not!'

'It's not fair!' shouted Diana.

When they went to fetch Margaret at home time, things were no better. Margaret and Diana quarrelled all the way home. They quarrelled in front of the television set. They quarrelled at the tea table. By the time Dad came in from work, Mum had had enough.

'I don't know *what's* got into them both!' she cried. 'They've been nothing but trouble for *days* now!'

'Come on, girls!' said Dad. 'What's the matter?'

'Nothing,' said Margaret.

'Nothing,' said Diana.

'Oh yes, there is!' said Mum. 'And what's more, you two are going to tell us what it is!'

Margaret and Diana sat at the table, and wriggled.

There was a very long silence. Then Margaret said, 'I don't want to go to school. It's not fair.'

'It's not fair *I* can't go to school!' cried Diana. 'She gets *everything*!'

'No, I don't!' cried Margaret. '*You* do! You and Mum!

25

You go to the shops without me! And you do the cooking without me! And – '

'You get climbing, and dancing, and books, and toys, and stories, and – ' cried Diana.

'Hold on a minute!' said Mum. And Dad said, '*Now* I think I see what this is all about! Margaret doesn't want to go to school because she thinks she's missing out on things Diana does with Mum. And Diana *does* want to go to school because she thinks she's missing out on things Margaret does there. And you're both feeling very angry with each other about it.'

'Well, it's not fair!' shouted both children.

'Little noodles!' said Mum; but she didn't sound cross any more.

Dad tried to explain things. 'Diana – you'll get your turn! And there are lots of nice things to do while you're waiting to be five. And Margaret – Mum still saves things for you and her to do together, doesn't she?'

Margaret nodded.

'In any case,' said Mum, 'it's no good you two blaming each other, and being jealous of each other! It's just the way things are.'

'Still,' remarked Dad, 'I'm glad you've said at last how you're feeling. Bottling things up inside yourself makes everything worse. Sometimes you can't tell *everybody*. But it's always a good idea to tell the people who care about you.'

'God cares how we feel,' said Mum. 'Why don't we talk to him about it?'

Margaret and Diana looked at each other again.

'All right,' they said.

'I'll be first,' said Margaret. She told God *exactly* how she was feeling. Then she asked him to help her to feel better. Then Diana and Mum told God how Diana was feeling, and asked him to help Diana to feel better.

Then they went on with their tea.

Margaret ate a large slice of cake. And she began to remember the times it was nice being older than Diana. Margaret was allowed to stay up a bit later. She could do quite a lot of things Diana couldn't manage yet. And it *was* fun at school, nearly always . . .

Diana ate another sandwich. And she began to remember the times it was nice being younger than Margaret. Diana could still ride in the pushchair when she got tired. Or sometimes Dad would carry her. And it *was* fun at home with Mum, nearly always . . .

But they still didn't feel quite happy.

When tea was over and cleared away, Dad suddenly said, 'Let's play bears!'

'Oh – I don't know,' said Mum. 'There are lots of things I ought to be doing instead of playing bears!'

'Yes! Yes! Let's play bears!' cried Margaret and Diana. It was ages since they'd all played together. And 'bears' was special. They'd made it up themselves, and it wasn't like anybody else's game of bears.

Mum looked at the three of them.

'All right,' she said.

So they rushed about finding furry things to dress up in. And they had a gorgeous game of hiding, and pouncing out, and growling, and laughing. And Diana and Margaret laughed so much they rolled on the floor together. And they were friends again.

Windy day

Outside, the wind gusted and howled round the school. Inside, Class One were supposed to be listening to a poetry programme. But they were very fidgety and noisy.

'It's a good thing I put this programme on tape!' said Mrs Dixon, when she had stopped the tape-recorder for the fifth time. 'Jivan – what *are* you doing?'

Jivan had been trying to reach a crayon which had rolled under one of the tables.

'Leave it for now!' said Mrs Dixon. 'We are all sitting and listening to *poems* at the moment!'

She set the tape going again. But next minute the wind blew so hard at the window-pane the children listened to that instead. Mrs Dixon switched off the tape-recorder.

'You've all got the fidgets because of the wind!' she said crossly. Class One sat very quiet, because Mrs Dixon was hardly ever cross with them.

Outside, the wind howled again. It buffeted against the school building, and whirled leaves around the playground. And Mrs Dixon said, 'It *is* hard to sit still on such a lovely windy afternoon. We'll go out and enjoy it! Come and get your coats on. You too, Paul.'

Excitedly, the children scrambled to do as she said. Soon they were ready, waiting by the cloakroom door. Mrs Dixon picked up a paper bag, and put it in her

pocket. Then she opened the door.

Whoosh! The wind tried to grab it from her. Laughing, she fixed it by its hook. And Class One stepped outside.

Oof! As they waited while Mrs Dixon closed the door, the wind tugged at them, and pushed at them, and made them laugh.

'Come on!' shouted Mrs Dixon above the noise of it. She took Paul's wheelchair, and began to run. Squealing, the children followed. All round the outside of the school they ran – not very fast – sometimes with the wind blowing them, sometimes sheltered by the school building.

Round the last corner came Mrs Dixon and Class One; and oof! the wind was right in their faces. Panting, they came to a stop for a moment. Then –

'Catch a leaf!' cried Mrs Dixon. And the children ran about, laughing and chasing the swirling leaves.

'I've got three!' yelled Pavan.

'I've got four!' cried Naima.

'Look at mine!' shouted Estelle. She had a big handful.

Mrs Dixon took out the paper bag. 'Put the leaves in here!' she said. 'We'll use them later.'

She gave the bag to Paul to hold. The children crowded round to put the leaves in, as well as they could for the wind.

Mrs Dixon looked at her watch.

'We've got time to walk to the top of the hill!' she said. 'Come on!' She took hold of Paul's wheelchair again. Laughing and squealing, the other fourteen children in Class One followed her out of the school gate. Along the pavement they went, feeling the wind at their backs, climbing, climbing all the time.

At the top of the hill there was an open grassy space.

The children turned around and around, feeling the wind in their faces or at their backs. They jumped up and down, while it tugged at them. They tried to stand on one leg; but the wind was too strong, and blew them over. They shouted; and the wind carried their voices away. They looked down and saw the trees and bushes in the school garden tossing their branches around.

'Time to go back!' said Mrs Dixon at last; and they set out down the hill. Now the wind was against them, making them puff, and pant, and push to get along.

At last they reached the playground safely. Into the cloakroom they went, talking and laughing and enjoying themselves.

Back in their classroom they rushed to sit on the carpet by Mrs Dixon's chair. Soon they were settled, ready to listen. Mrs Dixon sat down, her hair all wind-blown, her cheeks rosy.

'I did enjoy that!' she said. 'Didn't you?'

'Yes!' shouted Class One.

'Children,' she said, 'what does the wind look like? Which of you can tell me?'

Several children put their hands up. Then they put them down again.

'Did any of you see the wind?' asked Mrs Dixon.

'I did!' called Heidi.

'So did I!' said Richard.

And some of the others said, 'So did I!'

'Then tell me what it looks like!' said Mrs Dixon.

The children were very quiet.

'Did you *really* see the wind – or did you *feel* it?' asked Mrs Dixon.

'You can't see the wind,' said Paul.

'Is Paul right?' asked Mrs Dixon. Some of Class One had to think very hard; but in the end they all nodded.

'Yes. He *is* right,' Mrs Dixon smiled. 'The wind is

very real! But we can't see it. We can see what it does, though! For one thing, we saw it make those leaves whirl around! Have you still got them, Paul?'

'Yes,' said Paul, holding up the paper bag.

'Good boy,' said Mrs Dixon. And she showed Class One how to put a leaf on the table underneath a piece of paper, then colour carefully over it with a crayon to make the pattern of the leaf show through.

Soon the children in Class One were all busy making leaf patterns and pictures.

Estelle had especially liked the windy day walk. When she got home she told Dad all about it.

'We can't *see* the wind, but it's *real*,' she ended.

'That's right,' nodded Dad. 'And that very same thing is true about God! We can't see him. But he's real!'

Estelle thought about that for a moment. Then she nodded. 'Yes! We can't see God, but he's real!' she said.

Outside, the wind was still blowing. Inside, the room was warm and cosy. Estelle settled on Dad's lap to watch television. And she felt very safe and happy.

Harvest

One day Mrs Dixon said, 'It will be Willow Green School's Harvest Festival soon. Who knows what a Harvest Festival is?'

Class One wasn't sure. Mrs Dixon explained.

'We all need food, otherwise we'd starve. But *we* can't make things grow, ourselves! We can help. We can dig the ground and plant the seeds. But only God can make things grow. It's as if he puts some magic inside each little seed . . . Besides that, God planned the world so that it has day and night, sunshine and rain, cold weather and hot. Seeds need all those things to make them grow properly. So – every year, when the harvest of fruit and vegetables has been gathered in, we want to say thank-you to God. At Willow Green School we bring some of the best of our harvest things into the hall, and have a special service – like assembly. That's our Harvest Festival!'

The children nodded.

'Besides things to eat, we bring flowers, to say thank-you to God for making them so beautiful!' Mrs Dixon went on. 'Now – I wonder how many of you think you'll be able to bring something?'

'I will!' cried nearly everyone.

'Great!' smiled Mrs Dixon. 'And I wonder if any of you will bring something you've helped to grow yourself,

33

in your garden at home?'

Some of the children lived in flats, and didn't have gardens. But the others said, 'Yes!' And Okolo called out, 'I'll bring some potatoes!'

'I'll bring a marrow!' said Margaret.

'I'll bring some runner beans!' said Richard.

'I'll bring – ' began the rest.

'All right!' smiled Mrs Dixon. 'We don't want a list now! Let's wait until the day, then we'll *see*! Now – I've got a surprise for you! You're all going to have something you've grown in school to give to the harvest!'

Class One began to feel excited. They watched as Mrs Dixon reached into the large bag at her side. She brought out fifteen saucers (one for each of them), a wad of cotton-wool, and some small packets.

'Can you guess?' she smiled.

Class One couldn't.

Mrs Dixon tore open one of the packets, and tipped some tiny black things out into her hand.

'What are these?' she asked.

'Seeds!' cried Class One.

'Yes! Mustard and cress seeds,' nodded Mrs Dixon. 'Mustard and cress is lovely to eat in sandwiches, especially with egg or cheese. And it grows very quickly. Right! Let's get started! Come and get your saucer and a piece of cotton-wool.'

Excitedly, the children rushed forward. 'Ow!' cried Richard, pushing at Margaret. She'd trodden on his toe by mistake. 'Stop it!' said Margaret, pushing him back. 'Get off!' cried Pacho, as he bumped against her.

'Mrs Dixon!' cried half a dozen children, who were getting squashed.

'CLASS ONE!' cried Mrs Dixon. The children stood still. But two saucers had slipped to the ground and smashed. So Margaret and Richard had to wait till next day to plant their mustard and cress, when they could bring a saucer from home.

Mrs Dixon showed the others how to lay the cotton-wool on the saucers, and make it damp with a little water. Paul got too excited, and swamped his saucer. Sighing a little, Mrs Dixon gave him a fresh piece of cotton wool. 'But I won't be able to help you if you put too much water once the seeds are sown!' she warned. 'So be careful!'

Class One tried to be careful. The children each took a pinch of seeds and sprinkled them onto the cotton-wool. Then they put the saucers on the window-sills.

They remembered to water the seeds a little every day. The mustard and cress grew; and nothing else went wrong with it.

But other things went wrong. The nearer it got to Harvest Festival, the more things the children told Mrs Dixon.

'I was digging up my potatoes, and I put the prong of the fork right through the biggest one!' said Okolo.

'I've been watering and *watering* my biggest marrow!' said Margaret. 'And yesterday my mum took it by mistake, and cooked it for dinner!'

'Dad says our runner beans are going all stringy,' said Richard. 'And they're getting too big.'

'That's what *my* dad says!' said Joseph.

'Oh dear, oh dear!' said Mrs Dixon. 'And I was going to bring some chrysanthemums, but the frost seems to have got them, or something! Never mind! We'll all do the best we can. And remember – when we've had our harvest service, we give the fruits and vegetables to some of the old people who live nearby, and are our friends.'

On the day of the Harvest Festival, Class One came into school loaded down with harvest things. Most of the other children in Willow Green School had brought

things, as well. Each class in turn carried their harvest gifts in to Miss Westmore in the hall. They put the things onto a big table.

Mrs Dixon let Class One carefully cut their mustard and cress. 'It's our own harvest!' she smiled. Miss Westmore was especially pleased when she saw the mustard and cress.

The harvest things were arranged beautifully. By half past nine everything was ready for the Harvest Festival service. Some of the old people had been invited to come. They were sitting along one side of the hall.

Class One sat at the front. They saw everything. They smelled the lovely smells. They joined in with the hymns. They joined in with the thank-you prayers to God. And when the service was over, they were allowed to help carry baskets of the fruit and vegetables over to the old people.

'How lovely!' said the old people. 'Thank you, dears!'

Everyone was smiling and happy.

'I *do* like Harvest Festivals!' said Mrs Dixon.

'So do I!' cried everyone in Class One. And they sang a harvest song all the way back to their room.

James

It was playtime. James stood in the playground. All around him the other children ran, and shouted, and played together. James didn't have anyone to play with. He never played with anyone in the playground. And he was very frightened when the other children rushed about so noisily.

Mrs Dixon came out, carrying her cup of tea. She was on playground duty today. James moved across to stand beside her.

'Hello, James!' she said. 'Look! There's Paul over there! Wouldn't you like to go and play with him? I'm sure he'd let you.'

James looked across the playground. Paul was whirling his wheelchair round quite fast. And he wasn't even playing with other children from Class One. They were all bigger boys. James shook his head.

Mrs Dixon sighed a little.

'What about joining in with Amina and Aisha then?' she suggested. The two girls were sitting on the playground seat. They'd managed to find some daisies to pick in the grass round the edge of the playground, and they were making daisy chains.

James shook his head again. Sometimes bigger children came along and made the smaller ones get off the playground seat . . .

Mrs Dixon said, 'James, you've been in school for four weeks now! And you still haven't found out it's *fun* to play in the playground! You've never even given it a try! Go on! Have just one run round, then come back to me!'

James felt as if he was going to cry. Mrs Dixon looked at his face, and sighed again. But she stopped trying to make him leave her.

When *she* wasn't on playground duty, James stood beside whichever teacher *was*. And every day he hoped very much it would rain; because then the children stayed indoors.

Half term came and went; and still James spent all his playtimes standing close beside the teacher. So one hometime, while James was getting his coat on and looking for his outdoor shoes, Mrs Dixon spoke quietly to James's mum.

And after tea, while James was in the garden playing with his football, his mum spoke quietly to his dad.

That night, when James was tucked up in bed, Dad came in as usual. But before he started the bedtime story, Dad said, 'I hear you don't like playtime at school very much, son.'

James went very quiet. Dad said, 'I didn't like playtime when *I* started school, either.'

'Didn't you?' James looked at Dad; and he felt a whole lot better.

'I thought the other children would push me over,' said Dad. 'And there was so much *noise*!'

'I know,' said James.

Mum came in, and sat on the edge of his bed. 'Playtime *can* feel frightening, at first,' she said. 'But it's all right really, James. I'm sure the others are careful of the smaller ones.'

James shook his head.

39

'James,' said Dad, 'why don't we talk to God about this? We can always ask him to be with us, and take care of us when we're frightened or worried. He's promised he will.'

'Right,' said Mum. 'We know he loves us. So what we have to do is trust him and believe what he says.'

James picked up a book. 'I want this story tonight,' he said.

Gently, Dad took the book from him.

'In a minute, son. Listen – I'll tell you a different story. Once there were two little men who wanted to go to the seaside. They stood at the bus stop together. But when the bus came along, marked "To the seaside", the first little man said, "I'm not getting on *that*! I don't believe it *is* going to the seaside!"

'The bus driver said, "Oh yes it is! Truly it is!" But the first little man said, "I still don't think so." The second little man said, "There's only one way to find out!" And he got onto the bus.'

'Where *did* the bus go?' asked James.

'To the seaside,' said Dad. 'But the first little man never found that out. He never trusted anyone enough to give it a try.'

James thought hard. Mum said, 'Shall we talk to God now?'

'All right,' said James.

So Mum said a special prayer, telling God how worried James was about playtimes, and asking God to help him.

As soon as the prayer was finished, James had an idea.

'Mum! Can I take my football to school tomorrow?' he asked.

'Of course you can, if Mrs Dixon doesn't mind,' said mum.

Next morning Mrs Dixon smiled when she saw James and the football. 'I don't mind a bit!' she told Mum.

James carried the football into the classroom. He still felt upset when he thought about playtime.

'James! Can I play with you today?' asked Pavan.

James was surprised. Then he said, 'All right.'

At playtime James went outside, clutching his football very tightly. His heart was beating fast. But straight away Pavan came up to play with him. James put the ball down, and kicked it. Pavan kicked it back. Some of the others came and asked if they could play too. James said yes. And it *was* fun! Until – a big boy grabbed the ball and ran off with it.

It was *just* what James had been afraid of! He wanted to cry. But all the children who had been playing with him shouted, 'Hey! That's our ball!' And they all chased the big boy.

The boy looked round. He saw them – *and* he saw the teacher on playground duty noticing what was going on.

'I was only playing!' he said. He put the ball down and kicked it as hard as he could back to James.

James picked his ball up. For a moment he wanted to stand there, holding onto it, keeping it safe. Then he looked at the others rushing back towards him.

'Come on, James!' shouted Heidi.

James made up his mind. He put the ball down, and gave it a huge kick. The game was on again. And it *was* fun, playing with the others in the playground.

Class One's assembly

'Next Friday,' said Mrs Dixon, 'it's our turn to take school assembly!'

Class One felt very excited. Every Monday, Tuesday, Wednesday and Thursday, Miss Westmore the headmistress took assembly. All the children and their teachers went into the hall and sat down, while Miss Westmore stood at the front. She told them which songs or hymns to sing. She told them special stories. And she helped them to say prayers to God.

But on Fridays, one of the classes took assembly. *They* stood at the front, and did all those things – and other things as well. So far, everyone had thought Class One children were too small and new to take an assembly. But now Miss Westmore had decided they were big enough to manage it.

'What *we* have to decide,' said Mrs Dixon, 'is what our assembly shall be about! Let's try to think of something we want to say thank-you to God for.'

'Thank-you for pets!' said Aisha, remembering her pet dog.

'That's a good idea,' Mrs Dixon nodded, 'only Class Five thanked God for pets . . .'

'Thank-you for the sun!' said Paul, moving his wheelchair a bit further into the sunshine which streamed through the classroom window.

'That's another good idea,' said Mrs Dixon. 'Only Class Three did it . . .'

Class One frowned, they were thinking so hard. Mrs Dixon looked at her watch.

'Goodness me, it's time for swimming!' she cried. 'Come along, children! We'll have to think again when we get back.'

Class One hurried out to the cloakroom to get their swimming costumes and towels. Their school was very lucky. It had an indoor swimming pool. Soon the children were happily in the water, playing 'Here we go round the mulberry bush'. Mrs Dixon sang for them. Instead of the usual words, she sang ones she'd made up herself.

'This is the way we crawl along!' she sang. And 'This is the way we stamp our feet!' It was fun, crawling along in the water; or trying to stamp their feet, and making great big splashes. Sometimes she sang, 'This is the way we wash our faces!' And they could *really* get their faces wet. Or she might sing, 'This is the way we *run* along!' Or 'This is the way we jump up and down!' That always made a lot of splashing, too. But they were careful not to splash each other too much. Mrs Dixon had explained that some children didn't like that; and they wanted everyone to have fun.

Sometimes they sat down in the water, and wiggled their toes. Sometimes they tried crawling with their hands and letting their legs float out behind them. Sometimes Mrs Dixon let them wear arm bands. Then they could sit down, lean back in the water, and try to let their legs float up.

Paul joined in with some of the things they did in the water. Pacho's mum always came to help him especially. He loved being in the pool.

Joseph's mum always came as well. She helped Class

44

One to get undressed and put on their costumes. Then she helped Mrs Dixon to watch them while they were in the water. And she helped them to towel dry, and dress again afterwards.

Today playtime came after swimming. The children rushed about in the playground, and some of them got very hot. When Mrs Dixon saw their red, flushed faces she let them go and have a drink of water at the fountain. The cool water was delicious!

Presently the children were settled in their classroom again. And Mrs Dixon said, 'Class One, we really *must* decide what we're going to do about our assembly. What can we say thank-you to God for?'

And Heidi said, 'Water!' As soon as she'd said it, everyone knew it was a good idea. Mrs Dixon smiled.

'That's it exactly! Now – tell me what *you* especially like about water!'

Next moment she had to put her hands over her ears, as all the children called out at once.

'All right!' she laughed. 'One at a time! Margaret! You start! And when everyone's had a turn to say, we'll get out the paints and paint some pictures.'

On Friday morning the children in Class One were first into the hall. They stood at the front and watched all the other classes and their teachers coming in.

Miss Westmore came in last of all. She smiled at them, and sat down; and they were ready to begin.

First, everyone sang a song about raindrops. Then six children in Class One held up pictures they'd made, and Mrs Dixon explained that the pictures were about the way water gets into our taps.

Then Margaret pretended to be having a bath, with a plastic duck. Everybody laughed. Next, Joseph, Peter, Janice and Heidi pretended to be in a swimming pool, while Paul said a rhyme. After that some of the children pretended to be in a sailing boat at the seaside, while the rest sang a song.

Then, as Mrs Dixon told a story, Class One acted it. They were in a very hot country, and they were very thirsty. But there was no clear cool water to drink. There wasn't even enough water to wash themselves or their clothes.

At last Michael and Richard came along, and showed the others where and how to dig a well. Now there was plenty of water! But the children were very careful with it. It was precious.

When the story was over, it was prayer time. The children in Class One held up all the paintings they'd done to show what they especially liked about water. Then they said a special thank-you to God.

Everyone else joined in the 'Thank-you, God' prayer.

The assembly ended with a song about ducks enjoying the rain.

After the song, Miss Westmore said, 'Well done, Class One! That was a really lovely assembly! Thank you very much!'

And as Mrs Dixon and Class One watched the other children leading out of the hall, they smiled and smiled.

Richard

It was Monday morning. The children in Class One kept hopping up and down, looking out of the window. They were waiting for a fire engine to come and visit the school! It was going to park in the playground; and all the classes in turn were to be allowed to go out and look at it.

'Children!' said Mrs Dixon at last, 'You won't make the fire engine come any faster by peering out of the window! Let's have a news time while we're waiting. All of you – onto the carpet before I count five! One . . . two . . . three . . . four . . . four and half . . .'

The children laughed. They rushed to the front. And everyone – except Paul, who had to stay in his wheelchair – was sitting on the carpet as Mrs Dixon said, 'Five! . . . Right! Who has some news to tell?'

'I have!' said Richard. 'Yesterday I went to Junior Church!'

'That's nice!' said Mrs Dixon. 'What did you do there?'

'We had some singing,' said Richard. 'And we had a story. The story was about God always taking care of us, safe from being hurt.'

'That must have been a lovely story,' said Mrs Dixon. 'But Richard – does God *always* keep us from being hurt?'

'Yes,' said Richard, at once.

'Think!' said Mrs Dixon. 'Will God keep us from being hurt – whatever we do?'

'Yes,' said Richard again.

'Children – ' said Mrs Dixon. But before she could say any more they heard BEEEE BAAAA BEEEE BAAAA outside.

'It's come!' shouted Class One, jumping up.

'Sit down!' said Mrs Dixon. The children sat down.

'Now,' she said, 'we'll wait sensibly until we're told we can go out.'

At that moment, Miss Westmore opened the class-room door.

'If you'd like to take your class first, Mrs Dixon,' she said.

'Thank-you, Miss Westmore,' said Mrs Dixon. 'All right, children.'

Class One tried to be sensible; but it was hard, because they were so excited. The fire engine stood in the middle of the playground. Some firemen were there too, in their uniforms. The children were allowed to ask any questions they liked. And then – they were allowed to climb all over the fire engine! They were even allowed to climb up on top of it, as long as they used the little ladder at the back, where two of the firemen were waiting to help them. Another fireman waited specially to help Paul get out of his wheelchair and into the fire engine's driving seat.

Some of the children didn't want to climb to the top. But Richard did. He was very, very excited. And instead of waiting his turn, he tried to climb up the *other* ladder at the back of the engine, where no one was waiting to help.

'Richard!' cried Mrs Dixon. But she was too late. Even as the firemen turned round to see what was the

matter, Richard slipped and fell.

Mrs Dixon ran to him. He wasn't hurt much. But he was frightened. And he cried.

The other children stopped still wherever they were, because for a moment they were frightened, too.

'It's all right, Class One,' said Mrs Dixon. 'He's a very lucky boy. All he's done is scraped his knees and elbow.'

The captain of the firemen spoke very sternly.

'You see what can happen, children, if you get careless, and don't do what you're told!' he said. 'I've a good mind to make everyone get off the engine!'

Class One kept very still and quiet, except for Richard's crying.

'All right,' said the captain. 'You can go on having a look. But BE CAREFUL!'

Class One went on looking, being very careful indeed. Soon they were cheerfully asking questions and climbing about again. But Richard had to sit on the ground and watch, because of his sore knees.

When they went back into school Richard hobbled along to Matron's room. He came back to the classroom with a lovely bandage on each knee, and a big piece of sticking plaster on his elbow. He said Matron had told him off. And Miss Westmore was very cross with him.

The other children had still been talking about the fire engine, and the fun they'd had.

Now Mrs Dixon said, 'Children – before you go off and set to work – do you remember what we were talking about, before the fire engine came?'

Class One thought hard. But no one could remember.

'We were having news time,' Mrs Dixon reminded them.

'Richard said he went to Junior Church!' said Aisha.

'Good girl,' nodded Mrs Dixon. 'And – ?'

No one could remember anything more – not even Richard.

'I asked you a question,' Mrs Dixon said. 'Richard told us he thought God would keep him from getting hurt, whatever he did. Do you still think that, Richard?'

Richard's face went very red. He looked at his bandages and his plaster. Then he had an idea.

'Well,' he said, 'I didn't ask God. That's why I got hurt.'

Mrs Dixon shook her head. 'Children,' she said, 'suppose you prayed a special prayer – now – asking God to keep you from being hurt as you go home tonight. And then as soon as school was over, you rushed straight out of the gates right in front of a car that was coming down the road. The driver would try to put on his brakes. No use. You'd be too close to the car for him to stop. Would you get hurt?'

'Yes,' said Class One. They had been told that *many* times.

'So,' said Mrs Dixon. 'We ask God to keep us safe. But can we leave it all to him? Or do we have to do our part, and be as sensible as we can?'

Now the children saw what she meant. Mrs Dixon smiled at them. 'Like the fire-chief told you – we mustn't get careless!' she said 'All right! Off you go, and do some lovely fire engine pictures and stories for the firemen to see!'

And Class One did.

Christmas

It was only two weeks to Christmas! Willow Green School was full of excitement and bustle.

Some of the children were not specially excited, because their families had other celebrations, at other times. But most of Class One were very excited indeed.

'I'm going to get a bicycle for Christmas!' cried Richard one morning, as soon as he saw Mrs Dixon. The other children didn't wait for their turn to talk. They all shouted at once.

'I'm getting a whole *bag* of books!' cried Anna.

'Me and my sister are getting a swing for the garden!' called out Margaret.

'I'm getting a new football!' cried James.

Mrs Dixon put her hands over her ears.

'Stop! Stop!' she said. 'I can't hear *any* of you when you all talk at once!'

The children managed to be quiet.

'Now,' said Mrs Dixon, 'let's remember Christmas isn't only about *getting*! It's about giving, too. So let's go into the classroom, sit down quietly, have the register – and then think about the presents you're going to make to give to your mums or dads or aunties or uncles or grandparents or neighbours or friends. Then we'll get busy.'

Soon the children were hard at work. And by the end

of the week they'd made calendars, and Christmas cards, and cotton wool snowmen built round a tin so that you could put sweets in them if you wanted to, and a table decoration for Christmas dinner or tea.

The children who didn't have Christmas at home (because of the other celebrations they had) made everything except the cards, and enjoyed themselves very much.

And Class One didn't make just enough presents for their own families and friends. They made some extra ones as well.

Besides making presents, they decorated their classroom. And they learnt some Christmas carols. Their favourite was 'Away in a manger'. They sang it nearly all the time.

On one afternoon in the last week of term something very special happened. Nearly everyone at Willow Green School lined up, and walked across to the nearby church for a carol service. Paul came too, in his wheelchair.

When they got inside, they found the church was full of people. It was a good thing a space had been kept for the school children! Class One were in the very front row.

Some of the children from the top class were dressed up as Mary, and Joseph, and the inn-keeper, and the angels, and the shepherds, and the wise men. One child was the star. One was the ox. And one was the donkey. There was a manger, with real hay in it. There wasn't a real baby; but there was a lovely doll, ready to be baby Jesus.

When everyone was settled, the service began. All the people and most of the children joined in singing Christmas carols which told the story of the first Christmas. In between the carols, the children from the top class acted the story.

The angel came and spoke to Mary. Then Mary and Joseph and the donkey travelled to Bethlehem. The innkeeper told them there was no room in the inn. He showed them to the stable, where the ox stood by the manger. Baby Jesus was born, and Mary wrapped him in warm swaddling clothes and laid him in the manger.

That was where Class One had a carol to themselves. They stood up, and turned round to face everyone. Then they sang 'Away in a manger'. And they sang it *beautifully*.

After Class One's carol, the story went on. The angels appeared to the shepherds on the hillside. The shepherds came to the manger. Last of all the wise men came, following the star. And the wise men gave their gifts of gold, frankincense and myrrh to the baby.

It was nearly the end of the service now. Miss Westmore stood up, to say a prayer. And the children joined in.

'Thank-you, God, for all the happy times we have at Christmas. Thank-you for the presents we get, and the presents we give. And thank-you for giving us baby Jesus – the best present of all.'

Then everyone joined in singing the last carol, and the service was over. But the afternoon wasn't finished yet.

Class One danced back to school beside Mrs Dixon and Paul in his wheelchair. As soon as they reached their classroom, they fetched the extra presents they had made. Then Mrs Dixon took them along to the hall.

The hall was looking splendid. Glittering silver balls hung down from the ceiling. All along the walls were Christmas pictures the children had made. And in one corner stood a huge Christmas tree, sparkling with lights.

In the middle of the hall there was a long table covered

with a white cloth. On the table were plates of party food. But the party wasn't for the children. Coming in through the door at the other end of the hall were some of the people who lived near Willow Green school and were seventy years old or more. They were the same ones who had come to the harvest. They had been specially invited to come to the carol service, and visit the school afterwards. The party was a surprise for them!

When the people were sitting down, the children in Class One went round giving them a present each from the extra ones they had made. The old people were very pleased. And they said how much they'd enjoyed Class One's singing in the church, and could the children sing again – just for them?

So Class One sang all the songs and carols they knew, while the old people listened. And when the singing was over, the old people said it was one of the best presents they'd ever had.

The children hopped and skipped back to their classroom beside Mrs Dixon and Paul. And they all felt very, very happy.

Jonathan

Jonathan was worried. The children in Class One were going to play a reading game. But Jonathan *never* knew the answers. He just copied the others.

'Ready?' smiled Mrs Dixon. She held up a card with some words on it. The children began to hop, so Jonathan hopped.

'Good!' said Mrs Dixon. She pointed to the words. 'This card says "hop on the spot". What about – let me see – this card?'

She held up another one. Everyone sat down on the floor. Jonathan sat down on the floor as well. For the next card, everyone sat on a chair. So did Jonathan.

'Very good!' said Mrs Dixon.

Then came the next part of the game. Mrs Dixon held up one of the cards, and said a child's name. That child had to do what the card said, all by themselves.

Jonathan knew it *was* a game. No one got into trouble if they didn't get the word right. In fact, whoever Mrs Dixon asked nearly always did get it right. And most of the children sat up very straight *trying* to be chosen. Jonathan always sat very small.

He was even more worried about the words in books. Some of the children in Class One could read whole pages, without Mrs Dixon telling them *anything*. Jonathan couldn't see how they did it. He could only read one word. 'Jonathan'. And he was quite likely to get even *that* mixed up with 'Joseph', if he ever sat next to him while they were tracing their name cards.

He *wished* he could read. It would be *great*. And there were so many nice books in the book corner.

But it was no use. Whenever he picked up a book and tried to read it, he didn't know what any of the words were. Not one. he felt very stupid.

He didn't tell anybody. He just got more and more worried, until in the end he wouldn't go near books at all.

That didn't matter at home, because they didn't have many. Even at bedtime Jonathan usually watched television until he was sleepy, then Mum or Dad would carry him up to bed.

It didn't matter at Junior Church, either. Mostly the teacher there *told* a story; and the children drew pictures about it. They *did* have a paper to bring home. Jonathan knew there was a story on that. But he just put the paper straight into his toy cupboard, right at the back.

At school he never chose to go to the book corner. When Mrs Dixon read Class One a story he wouldn't even look at the pictures. But he couldn't stop himself from worrying. So he began to be difficult and awkward about other things. He stopped helping with the tidying-up. He even stopped wanting to arrange the things on the nature table; and that had been one of his favourite jobs.

Before very long, Mrs Dixon noticed. One day she sat down beside him and said, 'Let's read a story together, Jonathan! I think you'll like this one. It's about a long-distance lorry driver.'

'No!' cried Jonathan, jumping up. 'I *don't* like it!'

'But you haven't heard it yet!' said Mrs Dixon.

'I don't like it!' said Jonathan again.

'All right,' said Mrs Dixon. 'You go and choose a book you *would* like.'

Jonathan stood still, looking down at the floor. After a moment Mrs Dixon said, 'Jonathan – there are lots of things you're very good at. Did you know that?'

Jonathan looked at her with his mouth open in surprise.

She said, 'You're good at putting on your own coat, and doing up all the buttons. You can even tie shoelaces! If I want the flowers on the nature table arranged beautifully, I know you can do it. And when it comes to tidying-up – well, I just wish I had you at home to do my tidying-up for me there!'

She smiled at him. Jonathan began to feel a bit better.

'Don't worry if you can't read just at the moment!' she said. 'You've got lots of time! You're not even six yet! And even if you *never* learned to read, you'd still be just as important a *person* as anyone else! Just as good. Just as useful. Just as nice!'

Jonathan began to feel a lot better.

'Besides,' said Mrs Dixon. 'I think you'll be reading quite soon, if you give yourself half a chance! Look at this . . .'

She wrote a word on a piece of paper.

'It's the name of something we put on the nature table this morning,' she smiled.

Jonathan looked at the word. And -

'Does it – does it say – tadpoles?' he asked.

'It does,' she smiled. She wrote his name on another piece of paper. 'Show me which word says Jonathan!' she said. Jonathan pointed. 'And which word says – '

'Tadpoles!' cried Jonathan, pointing.

'Right!' she smiled. 'Come over to the book corner . . . Now – look – in this book – '

'It says tadpoles!' said Jonathan, in a whisper.

'It does!' she smiled. She left him in the book corner. Jonathan was going all through the book, finding the word 'tadpoles'. Or 'tadpole'. He could do it! He could read some words in a book! He could *really read*!

Jonathan looked at the tadpole book every day that week. He loved it.

When he went to Junior Church on Sunday he found they were having a book day. There were lovely books all over the tables. And there was one special book. A Bible.

'This is the book which tells us about God, and Jesus,' said the teacher, showing it to them. 'The stories I tell you on Sundays are in here, as well. Let's say a thank-you prayer to God for all the books we have – and let's thank him especially for the Bible.'

'Yes!' said Jonathan. He joined in with the prayer. And he added a little bit of his own. 'Thank you God because I can nearly read!' he said. 'Amen!'

Birthday surprise

Miss Westmore sat in Mrs Dixon's chair, and smiled at Class One.

'Mrs Dixon has to be away this afternoon,' she told them. 'I'll be looking after you till home-time, and Mrs Dixon will be back tomorrow. So – let's get started! How many of you have had a birthday since you started school?'

Eight children put up their hands.

'And how many of you will have a birthday before the holidays?' she asked.

Nearly all the other children put up their hands.

'I see,' smiled Miss Westmore. 'Who would like to tell me about their birthday? Paul?'

'I had a party,' said Paul, 'and my mum made me a cake like a bus, with candles on the roof!'

Class One laughed.

'Margaret?' said Miss Westmore.

'I had sixteen birthday cards!' said Margaret. 'And my little sister gave me a lollipop!'

Class One laughed again. Most of the children wanted to tell about their birthdays, although one or two said they didn't usually do anything special.

When everyone had had a turn, Miss Westmore said, 'Now I'll tell you a secret! Mrs Dixon has a birthday, too. And hers is – tomorrow!'

Class One were very interested. Miss Westmore went on. 'Do you think she would be pleased if you made her a card? And a present?'

'Yes!' cried Class One.

'I think so too,' smiled Miss Westmore. 'So let's talk about it!'

Happily, Class One decided Mrs Dixon would like one big card from all of them. And when they heard that Miss Westmore had brought some marzipan and some food-colourings with her in case they were needed, the children agreed that Mrs Dixon would like some marzipan sweets which they could make.

They set to work. They knew Mrs Dixon liked flowers. So every child drew a picture of a flower and cut it out, while Miss Westmore found a big piece of pretty green paper and folded it in half to make the card.

When all the flowers were ready, each child stuck the one he or she had made onto the front of the card. The rest of Class One watched, and said where they thought the flower ought to go.

Soon the card looked very pretty. Miss Westmore wrote 'A happy birthday to Mrs Dixon from Class One' inside, and all the children wrote their own names underneath.

They were very pleased when the card was finished.

Next, they all washed their hands. Then they spread clean white paper over the table tops. Miss Westmore gave everyone a small piece of marzipan, and came round with the colourings. The children chose what colour they wanted their piece to be. When the colour had been added, they made their marzipan into whatever shape they wanted. Most of the children made fruit shapes, but some of them made flowers.

Miss Westmore had brought an empty tin which was just the size they needed. Okolo put clean paper inside it.

When the sweets were ready, the children laid them carefully in the tin.

'We'd better hide the things!' said Richard. 'Else Mrs Dixon will see them when she comes in tomorrow! She comes in before us!'

'So she does,' agreed Miss Westmore. 'What about hiding them in my room for tonight?'

'Yes!' cried Class One. So they all went along with Miss Westmore, and watched her put the tin and the card safely on top of her cupboard. They chose Peter and Amina to be the ones to come and get them again.

Next morning Class One couldn't *wait* to get to school. In the cloakroom Mrs Dixon looked down at their grinning faces.

'What's going on?' she asked. But no one told her. Peter and Amina slipped quietly away to Miss Westmore's room. And when Mrs Dixon was sitting on her chair with the rest of Class One on the carpet around her, they came back – carrying the card and the tin of sweets.

'Happy birthday, Mrs Dixon!' shouted Class One.

'Well!' said Mrs Dixon. She looked at the card; and she opened the tin of sweets; and she was very pleased indeed.

'Thank you all very much!' she said. 'What a lovely surprise! The nicest I've ever had!'

The children grinned. 'Miss Westmore helped us,' they said. And they explained which flower *they* had done, and which sweet they had made.

Then Mrs Dixon said, 'This day has had such a special beginning – we'll give it a special ending, too! This afternoon we'll have a party!'

'Hooray!' cheered nearly everyone.

At lunch-time Mrs Dixon hurried out to the shop and bought a few things to eat at the party. And that after-

noon the children each made a paper hat for themselves, while Mrs Dixon made one for *herself*. They all laughed when she put her hat on.

They put clean white paper on the tables again. Then they played some party games. Everybody laughed a lot – even the children who had thought they didn't like parties.

When the games were over, they sat at the tables and had a party tea. It was only a tiny tea, because Mrs Dixon hadn't been expecting to give a party that day, and the shop hadn't had very much of the right sort of food.

When they had finished, and tidied everything up, Mrs Dixon said, 'Class One, what a lovely way this was to begin my new year!'

'Birthdays are nice when you share them!' said Paul.

'They are,' agreed Mrs Dixon. 'Listen – tomorrow we'll make up a prayer about them! We'll ask Miss Westmore to use it next time she has the birthday children out at the front in assembly!'

So they did. Their prayer said,

> 'For birthdays and for birthday fun
> That I can share with everyone;
> For days of rain and days of sun
> In this new year I've just begun;
> For happy sleep when day is done –
> I thank you, Heavenly Father.'

And Miss Westmore used it at every birthday assembly for the rest of the term.

Okolo

'I want to hurry up to school, Mum!' cried Okolo. 'I want to see the rabbit!'

Mum laughed. But she hurried up with Okolo. They reached school just as the bell went. Okolo quickly kissed Mum goodbye, and ran inside.

The rabbit had been given to Class One yesterday. They'd named her Lop-ears, and helped Mrs Dixon choose where the hutch should go – on one of the tables at the side of their classroom. Now they crowded round the hutch to have another look at her. She was eating a lettuce leaf. When she noticed the children, she stopped eating and twitched her nose. The children laughed.

'Come along!' said Mrs Dixon. 'Lop-ears is very beautiful, but she needs some quiet time to get used to us. And we do have other things to do this morning!'

Slowly, the children came away from the hutch to get on with their painting, and drawing, and writing, and building, and measuring, and weighing. But Mrs Dixon could see they were still thinking about Lop-ears.

'I tell you what,' she said. 'This afternoon we'll take her out to the school garden. She can hop about out there in the sunshine.'

'Oh, yes!' cried the children – especially Okolo. He loved Lop-ears already.

'But you'll have to watch her, so that she doesn't hop

right away!' warned Mrs Dixon.

'We will!' cried Class One.

They couldn't *wait* for the afternoon to come. But at last Mrs Dixon was carrying Lop-ears carefully outside, with Paul following in his wheelchair, and all Class One around them.

The school garden had a small lawn, and some flower-beds. On one side there were some bushes which Miss Westmore called the shrubbery.

Mrs Dixon put Lop-ears down on the grass.

The rabbit sat still for a moment, twitching her nose. Then she gave a few bunny-hops. Most of the children squealed.

'Sh!' cried Mrs Dixon.

'They'll frighten her, won't they Mrs Dixon!' said Okolo.

'Good boy, Okolo! Yes! That's exactly what they'll do!' agreed Mrs Dixon. 'Especially while she's so new to us.'

Okolo nodded. The children were quiet, watching Lop-ears. She began to nibble at the grass. 'Look, Mrs Dixon!' whispered Class One. 'She likes that!'

'*Wild* rabbits eat grass,' said Okolo. 'My gran told me.'

'Quite right,' Mrs Dixon nodded. 'And – '

She went on talking. But no one could hear what she said, because just then an aeroplane flew low over the school with a roar.

Everyone looked up at it, and some of the children pointed.

'My mum calls that the two o-clock jet, because it comes over every afternoon at two o-clock,' said Naima, when they could hear each other speak again. And then she cried, 'Where's Lop-ears?'

Everyone looked down at the grass. Lop-ears had

vanished.

'Oh dear! We shouldn't have taken our eyes off her!' cried Mrs Dixon. 'Search for her, children! She can't be far away. Quietly, now! And carefully! If you frighten her, it will make it twice as hard to catch her.'

With worried faces the children began to search.

'Suppose she gets out onto the road!' said Okolo.

'Or suppose a dog chases her!' said Joseph.

'Or suppose – ' began Aisha.

'Children – do stop supposing horrible things!' cried Mrs Dixon. 'Suppose we hurry up and find her!'

They laughed a little – but not much. They were too worried.

Okolo wanted to cry. There was a fence between the school garden and the road, but it was broken in places. The holes were quite big enough for a rabbit to hop through. He kept imagining Lop-ears getting really lost, and Class One never finding her again. And she was so little, and soft, and cuddly . . . He searched really hard. The other children were looking among the tall flowers in the flower-beds, being careful not to break their stems. Okolo began to peer under the bushes. And he saw a gleam of white fur!

'Mrs Dixon!' he called. 'She's here!'

Very gently he reached in, and pulled Lop-ears out into the sunshine again.

'Oh, well done, Okolo!' cried Mrs Dixon, hurrying to see. 'It's all right, children! You can stop looking! Okolo's found her!'

Proudly, Okolo carried Lop-ears back onto the grass, holding her the way Mrs Dixon had shown him. And he was so happy, he felt warm all the way through. The other children were very glad, too. For the rest of the time Lop-ears was out they watched her very carefully indeed.

When it was time to go back into school, Mrs Dixon let Okolo carry Lop-ears. Gently he put her back into her hutch. Before he shut the door, he bent down and kissed her.

'Nice little rabbit,' he said softly.

Gran came to meet Okolo from school that afternoon. Okolo asked Mrs Dixon if Gran could come in and see Lop-ears. Mrs Dixon smiled, and said yes.

'She truly is a beautiful rabbit!' Gran admired. Lop-ears sat up and twitched her whiskers.

'She knows me already!' said Okolo. 'I found her, this afternoon, when she was lost!'

And as they walked home he told Gran the whole story.

'Well!' said Gran. 'What a good thing you looked under those bushes, Okolo! That story reminds me of another one. A story from the Bible. Can you guess which one?'

Okolo thought for a minute. He had a Bible story book which Gran had given him. Whenever she was baby-sitting for him and his little sister she would read them stories from it.

'It's your favourite!' Gran said. Then Okolo remembered.

'It's the one about the lamb getting lost, and the Good Shepherd going to look for it, and never stopping till he found it!' he cried.

'That's right,' smiled Gran. 'He cared so much about that one lamb that was lost.'

'And now,' said Okolo, 'we know just how glad he was when he found it!'

'So we do!' said Gran. And they went happily on towards home.

Heidi

Assembly was almost over, and Miss Westmore was talking to the children before they went back to their classrooms.

'Remember,' she said, 'we're having our school concert at the end of next week. I hope you're all practising for it!'

'Yes, Miss Westmore!' said everyone. Class One said it very loudly. They were practising a play. So far, the play kept altering a bit every time they acted it. Mrs Dixon said she was beginning to get quite muddled; but she didn't mind as long as *they* knew what they were doing. They laughed.

That afternoon they practised their play again. It was about a boy who went out shopping with his mum. He didn't look where he was going. He ran into the road, and got knocked over. The ambulance came, and took him and his mum to hospital. There the doctors and nurses made him better.

When the accident happened and he got knocked over, someone had to phone for the ambulance. Usually, it was Okolo. Class One had a toy telephone; but it wasn't a very good one. It was small, and you couldn't really dial a number on it because the bit that moved round had come off. And there was no bell, either.

Heidi had a splendid telephone at home. It was almost

as big as a real one. It had buttons to press and made a warbling sound when it rang. So far, Heidi didn't have anything to say in the play. She was just one of the people out shopping who saw the accident happen. She *wanted* to have a better part; but there didn't seem to be one left over.

She began to think. If she brought her telephone to school, they were sure to want it for the play. Then *she'd* have to be the person who rang for the ambulance to come, because it was *her* telephone!

Mum said she could take the phone. So next morning Heidi came into school proudly carrying it.

'Heidi!' cried Mrs Dixon. 'What a gorgeous telephone! It's just what we need for the play! Is that why you brought it?'

'Yes,' smiled Heidi.

'That's very kind of you!' said Mrs Dixon.

Heidi looked at her. She wasn't quite sure what Mrs Dixon meant.

But when they practised the play again, and Heidi held onto the phone, Mrs Dixon said, 'Could you put the phone down on the table, Heidi? Then Okolo can get at it easily when he rings for the ambulance.'

For a moment Heidi wanted to cry. Then she felt very angry. She banged the telephone down onto the table. Mrs Dixon didn't notice. She was listening to about half a dozen other children who wanted to say something about the play. Frowning, Heidi went back to the crowd of shoppers.

And at home time she took the telephone home.

Dad had come to meet her.

'Hullo!' he said in surprise, when he saw what she was carrying. 'Is the play over? I thought it wasn't till next week.'

Heidi didn't answer.

'Heidi?' said Dad.

Heidi was quiet for a long time. Then she said, 'Well! *I* ought to phone for the ambulance, because it's *my* phone.'

'I see,' said Dad. They started to walk along together. Dad was quiet for a long time. Then he said, 'Heidi – are you feeling happy?'

'No!' cried Heidi. 'Because *I* ought to phone for the ambulance! Not Okolo!'

'I see,' said Dad again. They walked a bit further. Then Dad said, 'Heidi – are you sure that's the reason you're unhappy?'

Heidi didn't answer. She knew Dad thought she ought to share her toys. After a while, Dad said, 'Was Okolo pleased when he saw your phone?'

Heidi frowned. She didn't want to think about that. Because Okolo had looked *very* pleased when he saw the phone.

'I don't care,' she said.

Dad didn't say any more. They walked on together. Heidi had her tea. She watched television for a while. Then she played with her dolls' house. Before she went to bed, she put her telephone right to the back of her toy cupboard. There!

Next morning, Mrs Dixon said, 'Heidi, dear – have you brought your telephone today?'

'No,' said Heidi.

'Oh!' said half the class – especially Okolo.

'It's mine,' said Heidi.

'Of course it is,' said Mrs Dixon. 'We'd have been very glad to borrow it, that's all. Never mind, sit down, everyone.'

She started to call the register.

Heidi sat on the carpet feeling very cross. After a while she felt better. But when they practised the play,

she looked at the broken school telephone, and felt cross again.

Next week, Class One practised their play every afternoon. They'd almost got it settled now, and it came out practically the same every time. Heidi still didn't have anything special to say. And whenever she saw Okolo using the school telephone, she remembered *her* telephone. She began to feel very miserable.

No one said any more about it. But Heidi kept thinking . . .

On the morning of the concert, she went to her cupboard and pulled out the telephone.

'Heidi!' smiled Mum. 'Oh I *am* glad!'

Heidi still wasn't sure.

But Okolo was by the cloakroom door when she went into school.

'Mrs Dixon!' he shouted. 'Heidi's brought her telephone!'

Mrs Dixon came hurrying to see.

'Heidi! How kind of you!' she cried. 'Class One! Look! Heidi has brought her telephone after all!'

Then all the children cheered; and Heidi felt very happy. She danced into the classroom.

That afternoon Class One acted their play in front of the whole school. Okolo used Heidi's telephone. But Heidi was feeling so pleased and happy about everything, she didn't mind. And instead of staying at the back of the crowd of shoppers as she usually did, she came to the front. And when they were all pretending to wait for the ambulance she called out, 'Here it comes! Stand back, everyone! Make room!' in such a loud voice, the audience gave her a special clap.

And Heidi smiled and smiled.

Derek

Class One had a new boy. His name was Derek. And even on his first morning, he was a nuisance.

Miss Westmore and his mum brought him into the classroom.

'Here we are!' smiled Miss Westmore. 'This is Class One, and that's Mrs Dixon. Mrs Dixon – this is Derek Smith. We were talking about him yesterday. He's been to school for a while already.'

'That was before we moved house,' Derek's mum explained. 'Derek – you're to be a good boy at this school! D'you hear?'

She poked him. Derek shrugged crossly.

'I'm sure he will be,' smiled Mrs Dixon. Derek scowled. Mrs Dixon took him to see his peg in the cloakroom. Then his mum and Miss Westmore went away, and Mrs Dixon brought him back into the classroom.

'Now, Derek,' she said, 'what do you like to do?'

Derek didn't answer.

'Perhaps you'd like to come and see what we've got here,' Mrs Dixon said. 'Then you can choose.'

She took Derek by the hand, but he tugged himself free. So she let him walk round beside her. The other children were all busy. Derek looked at everything they were doing; but there was nothing he wanted to join in with. He didn't want to play with anything else, either. In the end Mrs Dixon said, 'All right! You sit at the colouring table, and draw me a picture.'

She got on with helping the other children.

Derek sat still for about two minutes. Then he scribbled all over his own piece of paper – *and* the piece of paper which Richard had been using.

'Get off!' cried Richard. 'Mrs Dixon! He's drawn on mine!'

'Oh, Derek!' said Mrs Dixon. 'You must *not* spoil other people's work! If you want another piece of paper, come and ask me! Richard – I'm so sorry! Could you possibly start again?'

'No,' said Richard, crossly.

'Well,' said Mrs Dixon. 'Why not go over to the maths table, and start on your maths work card?'

'All right,' said Richard. He liked maths.

Derek sat frowning, and wouldn't draw any more. Presently he got up, and went over to the children who were building a brick tower so that they could measure it.

CRASH! Derek pushed it over.

'Mrs Dixon!' called Estelle.

'I saw,' said Mrs Dixon, with a sigh. 'Derek! In this class we are *kind* to each other! We *don't* spoil what other people are doing! Do you understand?'

Derek looked cross.

At that moment the bell rang for playtime.

'All right, children,' said Mrs Dixon. 'Leave everything ready for when you come in. Now – who will look after Derek in the playground today?'

No one wanted to. In the end, Mrs Dixon took him out to the teacher on playground duty.

After playtime Derek still went on being a nuisance. He went on being a nuisance all week. He wouldn't sit still for stories. He wouldn't listen to news. In music he got hold of a drum and banged it so hard Mrs Dixon was surprised he didn't break it. He pushed Paul's wheelchair so that it almost ran off down a slope. If he wanted anything, he grabbed at it. If the others wouldn't let him have it, he hit them. And he was *always* saying he had to go out to the toilet just when everybody was settled.

Class One got really fed up with him. Some of them were even a bit frightened. No one ever wanted to play with him. And if anything went wrong, or something got lost, Class One began to say, 'Derek did it!' – whether he really had or not. So Derek got more and more angry, and spoilt things more and more. And the more angry *he* got, the more angry everyone else got. There were lots of quarrels, and people getting into trouble all day long.

On Friday afternoon, when Derek had gone out to the toilet as usual, Mrs Dixon said, 'Children! Listen! It's about Derek. I want you to help me.'

Class One looked at her in surprise.

'He just hasn't got used to school yet,' she explained. 'Miss Westmore says he didn't have a chance to go to a playgroup, as you all did. And he kept being away at his other school. He really doesn't *know* about sharing, and helping, and being friends. And I don't think he's very happy with us. Do you?'

The children shook their heads.

'So,' Mrs Dixon said, 'it's our job to try to *make* him feel happy. It's always our job to make new people properly welcome, isn't it! If we all try – and I'll try as well – I think we can do it! And as soon as he's happy here, he'll be nice to us. You'll see! Shall we have a go?'

'Yes!' cried Class One.

'Good!' smiled Mrs Dixon. 'That's all, for now.'

The classroom door burst open, and Derek came in. Straight over to the painting table he went, and grabbed a paintbrush from the blue jar.

Whoosh! Over went the jar of blue paint. The paint spilled everywhere.

'Derek!' yelled Mrs Dixon. Then she saw the other children in Class One looking at her. She took a deep breath, and started again.

'Derek,' she said quietly, 'I'm sure that was an accident. Next time, please remember to pick up the brush carefully. Now – I'll help you clear up the mess. Will anyone else help?'

After a moment, Naima said, 'I will.'

'So will I!' called half a dozen children.

'Great!' smiled Mrs Dixon. 'But one of you is enough. Who will you choose, Derek?'

For a second or two Derek looked at them with his mouth open. Then he said, 'Okolo.'

'All right,' said Okolo. He grinned at Derek. And Derek grinned back!

Soon the blue paint was mopped up, and Derek and Okolo were washing their hands together at the classroom sink. The children in Class One felt happier than they had all the week.

And so did Mrs Dixon.

Sports day

'It's a lovely sunny day,' said Mrs Dixon. 'Just right for our first sports practice! Come along, Class One! We'll go out to the field.'

The children left what they were doing, and came over to the door. Mrs Dixon picked up the bundle of hoops which she'd put ready there, and gave them to Richard and Jonathan to carry. The basket of balls she gave to Margaret and Amina; and the skipping ropes to Heidi and Derek.

'I can't skip!' said Derek, as he took hold of them.

'We shan't be using them for skipping!' smiled Mrs Dixon. 'You'll see. Are we ready? Off we go, then.'

Paul led the way in his wheelchair, and Class One went round to the field at the back of the school. Some of the children were feeling a bit anxious. They didn't know what they'd have to do. Mrs Dixon understood.

'This will be your very first school sports day!' she said, when they were all sitting on the grass. 'We always have a lot of fun! There will be some races specially for you. And there will be some for the older children. And of course, children in wheelchairs, or those who can't walk too well, will be able to join in some of the races. Grown-ups can come and watch, and there's even a race for them! We want everyone to enjoy themselves that day!'

Class One began to smile.

'All right!' said Mrs Dixon. 'Let's get started!'

The children scrambled up. Mrs Dixon arranged two ropes on the ground to make one long line. The children stood in a row behind the line, ready to run.

Paul wanted to be in the race too. There hadn't been any rain for ages, and the grass was so flat and dry he could move his wheelchair quite fast. So he lined up as well.

Mrs Dixon hurried some way down the field and laid two more ropes out straight on the ground, to show where the race ended.

'See who can be first across these ropes!' she called. 'Try to run in a straight line, and don't bump into each other. Are you ready?'

'Yes!' called the children.

'Then ready – steady – go!' shouted Mrs Dixon. And on the word 'go' Class One set off, racing towards the ropes as fast as they could go. But some of them were in such a hurry they tripped, and stumbled. And Paul was so fast in his wheelchair he got there before quite a lot of the others.

Richard was one of the first across the line. He jumped up and down. 'I won! I won!' he shouted. And he added, 'I'm good at running!'

'Richard,' smiled Mrs Dixon, 'We don't say things like that. We let other people tell us if *they* think we're good at something!'

'Oh,' said Richard.

'Besides,' she said, 'some of the others were just as quick as you! Lots of people won *that* race! Now – we'll have a *backwards* running race!'

Class One – and Paul – lined up again. This time when Mrs Dixon said 'Ready – steady – go!' they ran backwards. They began to laugh, and even more of them

fell over; but they didn't hurt themselves. Paul was laughing so much his wheelchair went almost round in a circle. Naima was first to finish.

'Naima's good at running backwards!' smiled Mrs Dixon. 'Now – we're going to use the balls.'

Class One had races with balls; and races with hoops; and races with ropes. They hopped, and jumped, and balanced. They went forwards, and backwards; and they even had a 'turning round and round on one spot three times' race, which Paul won.

In fact, every race was won by a different person. Some of the children didn't win any of the races; but they were good at other things – like cheering the loudest; or helping Mrs Dixon carry everything; and tidying everything up.

'Remember – the most important thing about sports day is that everyone shall enjoy it!' said Mrs Dixon. 'I'm sure *I'm* going to!'

'So am I !' cried everyone in Class One. And they couldn't *wait* for sports day to come.

By the time it did, all the children in Willow Green School had done a lot of practising. They'd got their mums and dads and uncles and aunties to practise, too. And they'd found out something.

When they went to assembly on the morning of sports day, Miss Westmore asked them about it. 'Did you find that you're all good at the same things?' she asked.

'No!' answered the children.

'Why do you think that is?' she asked.

The children thought hard. Miss Westmore helped them.

'Look round at one another!' she said. 'Are you all exactly the same?'

'No!' they laughed.

'Right!' she said. 'We're all different. God made us

that way. So of course we're all good at different things. It's just what you'd expect, isn't it?'

The children nodded.

'Suppose,' she said, 'we *were* all the same! We'd all want the same things at the same time! . . . Besides – suppose everyone was good at driving cars, but no one was good at making them? . . . Or suppose everyone's dad was good at cooking, but none of them were good at washing up! It wouldn't do at all, would it? Let's remember that, this afternoon! And for now – let's say a special thank-you prayer to God for making us all different!'

So they did.

That afternoon they all went out to the field for sports day. The children – and the grown-ups – had a splendid time. None of the children were naughty – not even Derek. Everyone joined in with the races. The teachers joined in when it was a race for grown-ups. And Miss Westmore won the egg and spoon race!

Class One raced, and cheered, and clapped, and enjoyed their first sports day very much indeed.

The wildlife park

Trying hard to be quiet and sensible, Class One and Class Two lined up, ready to get on to their coach. It was the last coach in a line of three. The children of Willow Green School were going on a trip to the Hazeldene Wildlife Park.

The coach driver helped Paul up into the coach. Then he folded up Paul's wheelchair, and stowed it away in the luggage compartment at the back of the coach.

'Come along, the rest of you!' said Mrs Dixon and Class Two's teacher, Miss Springfield. The children scrambled on. Some of their mums had come too, to help look after them. Everyone settled comfortably into the seats. Mrs Dixon put the bags with all their picnic lunches in them on to the luggage rack. Then she walked up and down the coach, counting everyone.

'Right!' she smiled to the driver. 'We're all here.'

'Fine,' he said, climbing into *his* seat. He closed the door, and started up the engine. Brrrm! brrrrm!

Mrs Dixon sat down next to Miss Springfield, and the three coaches moved off. 'Hooray!' shouted Class Two. Class One joined in. 'Hooray!' they cheered.

'That will do!' said Miss Springfield. But she didn't sound cross.

It wasn't far to the Wildlife Park. Some of Class One had never been there before. When they got out of the coach they stood very close to Mrs Dixon and Margaret's and Heidi's mothers, while the driver got Paul's wheel-chair out. Class One were all going to go round together, because they'd agreed that was what they would like best.

Mrs Dixon took charge of Paul, and they all set off along the path to the entrance.

The gate-man smiled at them and let them through without paying, because Miss Westmore had the tickets. Then they were on the wide path with animal enclosures along each side.

'Look at the tigers!' shouted Richard. Peter moved closer to Mrs Dixon. 'Can they get out?' he asked.

'No,' Mrs Dixon assured him. 'The park is quite safe, as long as we keep the rules, and don't tease the animals. Children – do you see how the tigers' orange and black stripes match the sunshine and shadow? That's a good thing, because it means they don't show up so easily in the wild.'

Class One nodded. When they'd finished looking at the tigers they moved on to the camels' enclosure. There was a notice on the fence. It said, 'These animals may spit.'

Class One laughed.

There were three camels – a father, a mother and a baby. The father certainly looked cross enough to spit.

'Look at their wide, flat feet!' said Mrs Dixon. 'Camels usually live in the sandy desert. Why would they need feet like that?'

The children thought hard.

'Have *you* ever tried to walk on hot, dry sand? Did your feet sink in?' Mrs Dixon asked them. The children nodded.

'The shape of camels' feet makes it easier for them to get along than it was for you,' she said.

'Why have they got humps?' asked Pavan.

'They can store fat in those,' said Mrs Dixon. 'That means they can manage for a long time without needing much food. They don't need too much water, either. That's a good thing, because food and water are scarce in the desert.'

The children were very interested. They moved on again, and came to the lemurs. They noticed how the lemurs used their furry tails to help them balance.

Then they went to look at the monkeys. They stayed a long time laughing at the monkeys, and noticing how they used *their* tails to help them hold on to a branch as they swung about in the trees; and how they had hands almost like the children's hands.

'I like the monkeys!' said Derek.

'I like *all* the animals!' said Heidi.

The children's legs were beginning to ache, so they sat down on the grass for a while. Then they went on.

They saw the giraffes with their long necks, and watched as the animals reached up to eat leaves from the tall trees.

They saw the brightly coloured parrots, who had come from countries where the sun was hot and bright.

They even saw some huge elephants. The elephants were using their trunks to take the buns people offered them.

Seeing the buns reminded the children they were hungry, and they hurried over to the picnic area.

The rest of the Willow Green School party was there already. The teachers and the mums handed out the picnic lunches, and everyone started to eat. The coach driver came and sat on the grass with them, and told them stories. He was fun.

After the picnic there was time for Class One to play on the climbing frame, slides and swings. Paul had a

great time on the swings.

Then the children went to look at the fish in the aquarium. And after that it was time to go back to the coach.

'Have you enjoyed yourselves?' asked the driver, as he put Paul's wheelchair into the luggage compartment again.

'It was great!' said Class One.

'Yes it was!' agreed Mrs Dixon and Heidi's and Margaret's mothers. 'And the children were so *good*!'

'Well done!' smiled the driver. Class One felt very happy. 'D'you know,' the driver said, helping the children into the coach, 'whenever I come to the wildlife park I always think how wonderful God must be, to have created all those different animals, and made them just right for the places where they live!'

'Yes!' agreed Class One. Class Two arrived, and climbed into the coach. The other children were in their coaches, too. Miss Westmore came round, to make sure everyone was all right.

Then the coaches set out for home. Brrrm! Brrrm!

'Let's have a sing-song!' cried the driver. He started them off. They joined in, and sang all the way back to school. And the coach driver sang the loudest of them all.

Janice

For a whole week Janice had been very quiet. Even
when Mum and Dad took her to the park on Tuesday
evening she didn't cheer up. At bedtime, Mum said,
'What's wrong, Janice?'

'Nothing,' said Janice.

'Oh yes there is!' said Dad. 'You're going round looking like a stewed prune in a thunderstorm!'

Janice grinned; but she didn't cheer up.

'Is it something at home?' asked Mum.

'No,' said Janice.

'Is it something at Junior Church?' asked Dad.

'No,' said Janice.

'Have you quarrelled with your friends?' asked Mum.

'No,' said Janice.

'Is it something at school?' asked Dad.

Janice began to cry. 'So that's it!' said Dad. He took
her on his knee. 'Come on!' he coaxed. 'Tell us!'

Janice went on crying. Mum looked worried.

'I'll go and see Mrs Dixon on Monday,' she promised.

'No!' sobbed Janice. 'I don't want you to!'

'Janice,' said Dad, 'when something's wrong it's never
a good idea to bottle it all up inside yourself. That will
only make things worse.'

'You have to find out what can be done to make things
better!' said Mum. 'And often the first thing to do is

talk about it to someone who cares about you.'

'We care about you,' said Dad. He reached over for the box of paper tissues, and gave one to Janice. 'Stop crying, blow your nose, and let's hear all about it!' he said.

After a minute or two, Janice managed to say, 'It's nearly the summer holidays!'

Mum and Dad looked at each other in surprise.

'I thought you loved having a holiday!' said Mum.

'Yes,' sniffed Janice. 'But after the holidays, Mrs Dixon said we won't be in her class any more.'

Dad said, 'You can't stay in Class One for ever! You're growing up!'

But Mum said, 'I see! You're thinking about your new teacher! Who will it be? Not Miss Grey? Is she going to take Class Two next year?'

Janice nodded, and nearly began to cry again.

'Who is this Miss Grey? Has she got two heads and a dragon's tail, then?' asked Dad.

Janice grinned a little. 'Of course not!' she said. 'But I don't like her.'

Mum said, 'Darling, you don't really know her! The children in her class like her, don't they?'

Janice nodded.

'Well, then,' said Mum.

'I still don't understand all this,' said Dad. Mum explained.

'One day Janice and some of the other children from Class One were in the school garden when they were supposed to have stayed in the playground because the ground was wet. Miss Grey was on playground duty. She found them in the garden, and was very cross.'

'I should think so!' said Dad.

'But she's *always* cross!' cried Janice. 'She's cross whenever she takes hymn practice. One day she made

Richard stand out in the front! And she shouts at the big ones!'

'I expect they deserve it,' said Dad.

'I don't like her!' said Janice again.

'I think you'll find you'll be all right when you're in her class, and you both get to know each other,' Mum said. 'But in any case, you don't want to spoil the whole summer thinking about it! Let's put it into our prayers tonight. And remember, pet, God will be with you always, wherever you are. He cares what happens to you. *He* cares even more than *we* do.'

'That's right,' nodded Dad. So they added a special prayer to their prayer-time. They asked God to bless Janice and *all* the children, when they went into their new classes. They asked him to help the children not to worry, but to be glad because they were growing up and moving on. And they asked God to bless all the teachers, too.

After the prayer Janice felt a bit better. She got into bed. Mum tucked her up. And before Dad had finished reading the bedtime story Janice was fast asleep.

She still felt a bit better when she woke up in the morning. This was the last day of term, and Mrs Dixon had promised they would have some fun.

Class One were in the middle of a game of Cat and Mouse when Miss Westmore opened the door and looked in. She said, 'Mrs Dixon – Miss Grey's ready now, if you are.'

Miss Grey? Janice went cold all over. But Mrs Dixon smiled.

'Yes, we're ready, thank you Miss Westmore. Children – listen! We're going along now to see your new classroom, and say hello to Miss Grey! Isn't that exciting?'

'Yes!' shouted nearly everyone. But Janice wanted to

cry. She went over to the door with the others. Mrs Dixon led them down the corridor. In two seconds they would be in Miss Grey's room . . .

Janice took a deep breath. Then she remembered her prayer. 'Please, God, take care of me!' she whispered desperately.

Mrs Dixon opened the classroom door. Miss Grey came to meet them. 'Hello, Class One!' she smiled. 'Come along in! This is where you'll be next term. It's a lovely room, isn't it!'

Janice followed the others into the room. And it *was* nice! The sun was shining in, and the room looked very bright and cheerful. The children in Miss Grey's class looked very bright and cheerful, as well! They were sitting on the carpet at the front, and they smiled at Class One.

'I'll be back in fifteen minutes!' promised Mrs Dixon. And she went away.

Janice wanted to run after her; but she was too shy.

Miss Grey said, 'We've left the chairs empty for you, Class One, so you can try sitting in them! Then I'm going to read you some rhymes till Mrs Dixon gets back. She's doing some last-minute adding up in the register.'

Paul arranged his wheelchair near the front. The rest of Class One scrambled for the chairs – and Miss Grey only said, 'Carefully, now!' in quite a kind voice. Janice settled herself. Miss Grey began to read. She'd chosen some funny rhymes. Everyone laughed. Janice had to laugh, too. And she began to feel a whole lot better.

Maybe next term would be all right after all!